P9-DTF-723

THE WIZARD OF OZ

TREASURY OF ILLUSTRATED CLASSICS™

THE WIZARD OF OZ

by

L. Frank Baum

Abridged, adapted, & illustrated

by

quadrum

Modern Publishing
A Division of Kappa Books Publishers, LLC.

Cover art by Carole Gray

Printed in U.S.A.

Contents

Chapter 1
The Cyclone 9

Chapter 2
Council with the Munchkins 17

Chapter 3
How Dorothy Saved the Scarecrow 29

Chapter 4
The Road Through the Forest 41

Chapter 5
The Rescue of the Tin Woodman 47

Chapter 6
The Cowardly Lion 57

Chapter 7
The Journey to the Great Oz 67

Chapter 8
The Deadly Poppy Field 73

Chapter 9
The Queen of the Field Mice 83

Chapter 10
The Emerald City! 91

Chapter 11
The Great OZ! 101

Chapter 12
In Search of the Wicked Witch 113

Chapter 13
The Winkies and the Winged Monkeys to the Rescue 133

Chapter 14
The Discovery of Real Oz 143

Chapter 15
How the Balloon was Launched 155

Chapter 16
Away to the South 161

Chapter 17
The Lion Becomes the King of Beasts 171

Chapter 18
The Country of the Quadlings 177

Chapter 19
Glinda the Good Witch Grants Dorothy's Wish 183

About the Author 189

Chapter 1

The Cyclone

Dorothy lived in the Kansas countryside with her Uncle Henry, a farmer, and her Aunt Em. They lived in a small house on a large farm. Before Dorothy arrived on the farm, her aunt and uncle lived very quiet lives with nothing to smile about. She brought laughter

into their dull lives. Dorothy had a dog called Toto. He was a little black dog, with long, silky hair and eyes that twinkled happily.

One day, Uncle Henry sat upon the doorstep along with Dorothy and Toto and looked up at the sky. From the far north, they heard the low sound of the wind, they could see the grass moving back and forth. The wind grew stronger and the movements of the grass became faster.

Suddenly Uncle Henry stood up.

"What's wrong, Uncle Henry?" cried Dorothy.

Uncle Henry told her to get back in the house. He ran to the kitchen, where Aunt Em was washing dishes.

"There's a cyclone coming! I'll go outside and get the animals settled in," Uncle Henry told his wife. He then ran to the sheds where the horses and cows were kept.

Aunt Em dropped the plate she had in her hand and called out to Dorothy, "Quick, Dorothy! Run for the cellar!"

Toto, who was frightened, jumped out of Dorothy's arms and hid under the bed. Dorothy ran to get him. Aunt Em, who was very frightened, ran outside the house. She threw open the trapdoor in the floor and climbed down the ladder into the small, dark hole to get to the cellar where they would go when a cyclone came.

Dorothy finally managed to get a hold of Toto. As she was about to leave the house, there

was a great shriek of wind that came from outside the house. Then a strange thing happened. The house whirled around two or three times and rose slowly through the air. Dorothy felt as if she were going up in a balloon.

Suddenly, the house began shaking so violently that Dorothy lost balance and fell to the floor. She somehow picked herself up and took herself and Toto to her bed. The cyclone carried the house and spun it a few times. The great pressure of the wind on every side of the house raised it up higher and higher, until it was at the very top of the cyclone and was carried miles and miles away as easily as you could carry a feather.

It was very dark, and the wind howled horribly around her, but

Dorothy found she was riding quite easily. After the first few whirls, she felt as if she were being rocked gently, like a baby in a cradle, and eventually fell asleep.

Chapter 2

Council with the Munchkins

A sudden and severe shock woke Dorothy. She realized that the house was not moving, so she jumped from her bed and ran to the front door. What she saw when she opened the front door amazed her beyond belief.

The cyclone had set the house down, without any damage, in a beautiful country. There were lovely patches of garden all about, with stately trees bearing rich and luscious fruits. Plenty of gorgeous flowers were on every tree and bush, and birds with rare and brilliant

plumage sang and fluttered in the trees and bushes. A little way off was a small brook, rushing and sparkling along between green banks.

As she admired the scene around her, she saw a group of strange people coming toward her. The little men weren't as tall as Dorothy, but were far older than even her Uncle Henry! There was a woman of normal height with them. As they drew near the house, the group stopped to whisper amongst themselves. Then, the woman stepped forward and sweetly spoke to Dorothy. "Noble Sorceress, welcome to the land of the Munchkins! We are forever grateful to you for having killed the Wicked Witch of the East. You have freed us."

Dorothy looked at her, very confused. She didn't understand a word that was said to her. How could she, an innocent girl from Kansas, be called a sorceress? She replied back, hesitantly, "You are very kind. But you

are also mistaken. I haven't killed anybody!"

"Your house did," replied the woman, laughing, "That is the same thing! Look!" She pointed to a corner of the house. "Those are her feet sticking out from under your house." Dorothy gave a cry of dismay, for there were indeed two feet sticking out, clad in silver slippers.

Dorothy started panicking. "Oh, dear! The house fell on her! Whatever shall we do?"

"Nothing can or shall be done," said the woman calmly. "The Wicked Witch of the East made the Munchkins her slaves for many years. Now, thanks to you, they are free."

"Who are the Munchkins?" asked Dorothy.

"They are the people who live here, in the Land of the East," replied the woman.

"Are you a Munchkin?" asked Dorothy curiously.

"No, I am their friend. I live in the Land of the North. I came swiftly when I heard about the Witch of the East. I am the Witch of the North."

"A real witch?" asked Dorothy, with eyes open wide.

"Yes," replied the woman, "I am a good witch, and the people love me. I am not as powerful as the Witch of the East or I would've set them free myself."

Dorothy told her that she thought all witches were bad.

"You are mistaken," said the woman, "for there are only four witches in the Land of Oz. The Witches of the North and South are good witches. You have killed one of the bad ones, the Witch of the East. There is also the Witch of the West. She's worse than the Witch of the East!"

"But I've been told that witches don't exist anymore!" exclaimed Dorothy.

"In civilized countries, they don't. But the Land of Oz is cut off from the rest of the world," said the woman.

"Do wizards also exist?" asked Dorothy. "And who is Oz?"

"Of course they exist! Oz himself is a great wizard. He lives in the Emerald City. He is more powerful than all four of us witches together."

Just then, the Munchkins who had been standing silently gave a loud shout, and pointed to where the Wicked Witch lay. Her feet had disappeared completely, leaving behind only the silver slippers.

"She was so old that she dried up in the sun," explained the Witch of the North.

She picked up the slippers and gave them to Dorothy, telling her that they now belonged to her. One of the Munchkins added that there was a charm to the slippers that no one knew of. Dorothy spoke to the Witch of the North, "I want to go back to my Uncle Henry and Aunt Em. Can you help me find my way back?" The Munchkins and the witch shook their heads.

Dorothy began to weep, for she felt very lonely among these strange people. The witch took off her cap, and after saying, "One, two, three!" the cap suddenly changed into a slate, on which was beautifully written:

Let DOROTHY go
to the City of EMERALDS

"Is your name Dorothy?" asked the witch. Dorothy nodded, drying her eyes.

"Then you must go to the Emerald City. Perhaps Oz will be able to help you."

"Where is the Emerald City?" asked Dorothy.

"In the center of the country. It is ruled by Oz himself."

"How do I get there?"

"You must walk. You may come across good things and bad things. However, I will use my magic to protect you. No one can harm someone who has been kissed by the Witch of the North," said the witch.

With that, she kissed Dorothy on her forehead, leaving a shining mark.

"The road to the Emerald City is paved with yellow bricks. Tell Oz your story and ask him to help you." The good witch then blew a kiss at Dorothy. "Good-bye and good luck," she said.

The three Munchkin men disappeared through the trees. The witch spun on her left heel three times and also disappeared. Dorothy was left alone and hungry, and upon seeing the delicious fruit hanging from the trees, decided that she would make them her breakfast, also picking a few more for her journey.

Chapter 3

How Dorothy Saved the Scarecrow

Dorothy dressed herself in the only clothes she had left, a blue and white checked pinafore. Then she looked down at her feet and noticed how old and worn her shoes were.

"They surely will never do for a long journey, Toto," she said. At that moment Dorothy saw lying on the table the silver slippers that had belonged to the Witch of the East.

"I wonder if these slippers will fit me," she said to Toto. "They would be just the thing to take a long walk in, for they could not wear out."

She took off her old leather shoes and tried on the silver ones, which fit her as well as if they had been made for her.

"Come along, Toto," she said. "We will go to the Emerald City and ask the Great Oz how to get back to Kansas again."

Within a short time she was walking briskly toward the Emerald City, her silver slippers tinkling merrily on the hard, yellow road. The sun shone bright, and the birds sang sweetly.

Toward evening, Dorothy came

across a house much larger than the rest. She thought she'd go and ask for shelter there. She came to the front lawn and saw many men and women dancing. They were celebrating the death of the Wicked Witch.

The man of the house, Boq, attended to Dorothy himself, and gave her and Toto a hearty dinner. When Boq saw her slippers, he

remarked, "You must be a powerful sorceress." Dorothy looked at him questioningly. "You have killed the Witch of the East, and you wear her slippers! Plus, your frock has white in it. Only witches or sorceresses wear white."

"My dress is blue and white checked," said Dorothy.

"It is kind of you to wear that. Blue is the color of the Munchkins, white is the witch's color. We know that you are a good witch," said Boq.

The Munchkins told her that the journey would take her many days. She would come across good things and bad in this beautiful country.

This worried Dorothy a bit, but she consoled herself with the thought that Oz would help her get back to Kansas. She said good-bye to her friends and continued down the yellow brick road.

After several miles, she stopped and sat on top of a fence to rest her poor feet. There was a great cornfield beyond the fence, and not far away she saw a Scarecrow, placed high on a pole to keep the birds from the ripe corn.

He was raised above the stalks of corn by means of the pole stuck up his back.

As she looked intently at him, she thought she saw him wink at her. She blinked back in confusion. The Scarecrow then gave her a friendly nod. She jumped off the fence and went straight to him. "Good day," the Scarecrow said to her.

"Did you speak?" asked Dorothy, with her eyes wide open.

"Yes," he replied. "How do you do?"

"Very well, thank you," she replied. "And you?"

"Not too well," said the Scarecrow with a smile. "It is difficult being perched on this pole all day and night to scare the crows away."

"Can't you get down?" asked Dorothy.

"No, the pole is stuck up my back. Can you get me off it?"

Dorothy managed to get the Scarecrow down from the pole, as he was very light. Once his feet touched the ground, he started thanking her profusely. He then began walking a bit awkwardly beside her.

"Who are you?" he asked. "Where are you off to?"

"I'm Dorothy, and I'm on my way to the Emerald City. I am going there to meet the Great Oz."

"Where is the Emerald City? And who is Oz?"

"You don't know?" asked Dorothy, surprised.

"No, I don't. I am filled with straw all over. I have no brains," he said sadly.

"I'm so sorry," said Dorothy.

"Hey, do you think if I go to the Emerald City, Oz would give me some brains?" the Scarecrow asked hopefully.

"I don't know," replied Dorothy. "You may come with me, if you like. Even if he doesn't give you any brains, you'll not be worse off than you are now."

"True. You see, I don't mind my legs and arms and body being stuffed, because I cannot get hurt. If anyone steps on my toes or sticks a pin into me, it doesn't matter, for I can't feel it. But I do not want people to call me a fool, and if my head stays stuffed with straw instead of with brains, as yours is, how am I ever to know anything?" he asked.

"Come with me, then. I will ask Oz to help you," said Dorothy.

"Oh, thank you!" cried the Scarecrow with joy.

They walked back to the yellow brick road, and Dorothy helped the Scarecrow across the fence. Toto, who didn't like the new member of their group, started barking at him. Dorothy reassured the Scarecrow that Toto was quite friendly and that he did not bite.

"That's all right," said the Scarecrow. "Even if he did, it wouldn't hurt me. I am not afraid. There is just one thing that I am really and truly afraid of."

"What is it?" asked Dorothy.

"A lit match."

Chapter 4

The Road Through the Forest

Walking down the road after a few hours became a bit of a problem, for the Scarecrow kept stumbling over the yellow bricks, which were uneven. At noon, they stopped by a brook for some rest. Dorothy took out some bread from

her basket and offered it to the Scarecrow. He refused, saying that he was never hungry, for his mouth was filled with straw.

"Tell me something about yourself and where you are from," he asked Dorothy. After she ate, she told him all about Kansas, the cyclone, and how it had brought her to this country. The Scarecrow asked her why she would want to leave such a beautiful country to go back to someplace dry and gray like Kansas.

"There is no place like home," replied Dorothy sadly. "Tell me something about yourself while we rest."

"I've had a very short life. I was made only the day before yesterday! The farmer carried me under his arm to the cornfield and set me up on a tall stick, where you found me. I tried to follow him, for I hated being deserted like this. But my feet would not touch the ground. So there I remained. Many crows flew near me, but they flew away immediately, as they thought I was a Munchkin.

But then, an old crow came, and after he perched on my shoulder he realized that I was not a Munchkin, that I was made of straw. So he ate all the corn he could."

"I felt sad at this, for it showed I was not such a good Scarecrow after all. But the old crow comforted me, saying, 'If you only had brains in your head, you would be as good a man as any of them, and a better man than some of them.' A brain is the only thing worth having in this world, no matter whether one is a crow or a man."

"Once the crow left, I decided to try hard and get me some brains. From what you've said, the Great Oz will surely give me the brains I need!"

"I hope so," said Dorothy earnestly, "since you seem anxious to have them. Let us go." And she handed the basket to the Scarecrow.

Toward the evening they came to a great forest, where the trees grew so big and close together that their branches met over the road of yellow bricks. It was almost dark under the trees, for the branches shut out the daylight. They soon found themselves stumbling along in the darkness.

"If you see any house or any place where we can pass the night," Dorothy said, "you must tell me, for it is very uncomfortable walking in the dark."

So the Scarecrow led her through the trees until they reached

a cottage, and Dorothy entered and found a bed of dry leaves in one corner. She lay down at once, and with Toto beside her, soon fell into a sound sleep. The Scarecrow, who was never tired, stood up in another corner and waited patiently until morning came.

Chapter 5

The Rescue of the Tin Woodman

When Dorothy woke up, she was startled by a loud groan coming from the trees.

"What was that?" she asked timidly.

"I don't know. Let's go see," said the Scarecrow.

Just then another groan reached their ears. The sound seemed to come from behind them. They turned and walked through the forest. Dorothy discovered something shining in a ray of sunshine that fell between the trees. She ran to the place, and then stopped short with a little cry of surprise.

One of the big trees had been partly chopped through, and standing beside it, with an ax lifted in his hands, was a man made entirely of tin. His head, arms, and legs were joined to his body, but he stood perfectly motionless. Dorothy looked at him in amazement, and so did the Scarecrow, while Toto barked sharply.

"Did you just groan?" asked Dorothy.

"Yes," answered the Tin Woodman, "I did. I've been groaning for more than a year, and no one has ever heard me before or come to help me."

"What can I do for you?" she inquired softly.

"Get an oil can and oil my joints," he answered. "They are rusted so badly that I cannot move them at all; if I am well oiled I shall soon be all right again. You will find an oil can on a shelf in my cottage."

Dorothy at once ran back to the cottage and found the oil can, and then she returned and asked anxiously, "Where do I apply it?"

"Oil my neck first," said the Tin Woodman. His neck was so rusted that the Scarecrow had to hold his head and slowly turn it from one side to another so that the Tin Woodman wouldn't hurt himself. "Now oil the joints in my arms," he said. And Dorothy oiled them and the Scarecrow bent them

carefully until they were quite free from rust and as good as new. The Tin Woodman gave a sigh of satisfaction and lowered his ax, which he leaned against the tree.

"Oh! That feels good," he said with a sigh of relief. "I've been holding up that ax for more than a year. Now, if you will oil the joints of my legs, I shall be all right once more." So they oiled his legs until he could move them freely; and he thanked them again and again for his release.

"You have certainly saved my life. How did you happen to be here?" he asked.

"We are on our way to the Emerald City to see the Great Oz," Dorothy answered.

"Why do you wish to see Oz?" he asked.

"I want him to send me back to Kansas, and the Scarecrow wants him to put a few brains into his head," she replied.

The Tin Woodman fell quiet for a minute, as if in deep thought. He said to Dorothy, "Do you suppose Oz could give me a heart? If you will allow me to join your party, I will also go to the Emerald City and ask Oz to help me," he said.

Dorothy and the Scarecrow heartily agreed. The Tin Woodman picked up his ax and they all made their way through the trees until they found the yellow brick road again. Dorothy had carried the oil can in her basket, in case the Tin Woodman got rusted again.

It was a good thing that they had the Tin Woodman with them. Soon after they resumed their journey, they came across trees and branches so thick that it made it impossible for them to pass through. But the Tin Woodman took up his ax and chopped at the trees until he made a clear path for them.

As they continued walking, the Tin Woodman began to tell them his story. "I was born to a woodcutter. I fell in love with one of the Munchkin girls. I wanted to marry her. But she lived with an old woman, who didn't want her to marry and leave. So, the old woman went to the Wicked Witch of the East and asked her to prevent the marriage. The witch enchanted my ax. The ax started slipping while I was chopping wood, and it cut my body parts one by one. I got them replaced from a tinsmith. Soon, my entire body was made of tin, but, alas! I now had no heart, so I lost all my love for the Munchkin girl, and did not care whether I married her or not."

"The one thing that bothered me was the joints getting rusted. That's why I kept an oil can on the shelf in the cottage and made sure I oiled my joints regularly. But one day, I forgot to do so, and on that very day I was caught in a rainstorm. I rusted immediately.

And that was how I stood, until you found me! I want to ask Oz for a heart. If he gives me one, I will come back and marry the Munchkin girl."

Both Dorothy and the Scarecrow had been greatly interested in the story of the Tin Woodman, and now they knew why he was so anxious to get a new heart.

What worried Dorothy most was that the bread was nearly gone, and another meal for her and Toto would empty the basket. Neither the Woodman nor the Scarecrow ever ate anything, but she and Toto were not made of tin or straw, and could not live unless they were fed.

Chapter 6

The Cowardly Lion

All this time Dorothy and her companions had been walking through the thick woods. The road was still paved with yellow bricks, but these were completely covered by dried branches and dead leaves from the trees, and the walking was not at all good.

Now and then there came a deep growl from some wild animal hidden amongst the trees. These sounds made Dorothy's heart beat fast, for she did not know what made them, but Toto knew, and he walked close to Dorothy's side, not even barking in return.

"How long will it be," she asked of the Tin Woodman, "before we are out of the forest?"

"I don't know," he replied. "I have never been to the Emerald City. The journey there is dangerous. But I am not afraid, as long as I have my oil can. Nothing can hurt the Scarecrow. You are protected by the good witch's kiss mark on your forehead."

"What about Toto?" she cried. "Who will protect him?"

"We will protect him ourselves if he is in danger."

Just as he spoke, there came from the forest a terrible roar, and the next moment a great Lion bounded onto the road. With one blow of his paw, he sent the Scarecrow spinning over the edge of the road, and then he struck at

the Tin Woodman with his sharp claws. But, to the Lion's surprise, he could make no impression on the tin, although the Tin Woodman fell over on the road and lay still.

As the Lion turned toward Toto, he opened his jaws to bite the little barking dog. Dorothy, who was scared that Toto would be killed, ran forward without thinking, and slapped the Lion hard on his nose. She cried out, "Don't you dare bite Toto! You ought to be ashamed of yourself, a big beast like you, biting a poor little dog!"

"I didn't bite him," said the Lion as he rubbed his nose with his paw where Dorothy had hit him.

"No, but you tried to," she retorted. "You are nothing but a

big coward."

"I know it," said the Lion, hanging his head in shame. "I've always known it. But how can I help it?"

"I don't know, but how can you strike a stuffed man like Scarecrow?"

"He's stuffed?" he asked,

surprised. He saw Dorothy pick up the lopsided Scarecrow and pat him in shape.

"Of course he's stuffed," replied Dorothy, who was still angry.

"So that's why he fell easily," remarked the Lion. "I was surprised to see how fast he whirled and fell. Is the other one stuffed, too?"

"No," replied Dorothy, frowning, "he's made of tin." She helped the Tin Woodman up.

"That's why he nearly made my claws blunt! When they scratched against his tin chest, I got shivers down my back." He looked at Toto. "What is that little animal you are so fond of?"

"He is my dog, Toto," answered Dorothy.

"Is he made of tin, or stuffed?" asked the Lion.

"Neither. He's a—a—a meat dog," said the girl.

"He is quite small for someone who bites! No one would think of biting something that small, except a coward like me," said the Lion, hanging his head shamefully.

"What makes you a coward?" asked Dorothy, looking at the great beast in wonder, for he was as big as a small horse.

"I suppose I was born that way. All the other animals in the forest naturally expect me to be brave, for the Lion is the King of Beasts. I learned that if I roared very loudly, every living thing was frightened, and got out of my way.

"Whenever I've met a man, I've been awfully scared; but I just roar at him, and he always runs away as fast as he can go. If the elephants and the tigers and the bears had ever tried to fight me, I would have run myself, but I'm such a coward; just as soon as they hear me roar, they all try to get away from me, and of course I let them go."

"But that isn't right. The King of Beasts shouldn't be a coward," said the Scarecrow.

"I know it," returned the Lion, wiping a tear from his eye with the tip of his tail. "It is my great sorrow, and makes my life very unhappy. But whenever there is danger, my heart begins to beat fast."

"Do you have a heart disease?" asked the Tin Woodman. The Lion shook his shaggy head. "If you do, be glad, for it shows that you still have a heart. I don't have a disease because I don't have a heart. I'm going to the Great Oz to ask him for a heart."

"And I'm going to ask him for some brains!" added the Scarecrow.

"I'll be asking him for a way to send me and Toto back to Kansas," said Dorothy.

"Do you think Oz could give me courage?" asked the Cowardly Lion.

They nodded in agreement.

"Then, if you don't mind, I'll go with you," said the Lion, "for my life is simply unbearable without a bit of courage."

They happily welcomed him. Toto did not like this at all, for he still remembered how the Lion tried to bite him. But after a while, he got close to the Lion and they became good friends.

Chapter 7

The Journey to the Great Oz

They slept under a large tree that night. The next morning, they continued to the Emerald City.

They found the forest very thick, and it looked dark and gloomy. To add to their discomfort, they soon heard strange noises, and the Lion whispered to them that it was in this part of the country that the Kalidahs lived.

"What are they?" asked Dorothy.

"They are monstrous beasts with bodies like bears and heads like tigers," replied the Lion.

At that point they came across a large gap in the road. They weren't sure how they would cross it until the Lion realized that he could jump across it with each of

his friends on his back, one after the other.

Dorothy went first, with Toto on her lap, followed by the Tin Woodsman and the Scarecrow, until they were all on the other side.

They soon came across another gap in the road, this one so broad that even the Lion wouldn't have been able to jump across.

The Scarecrow looked around, and then said, "Here is a great tree, standing close to the ditch. Tin Woodman can chop it down so that it will fall to the other side."

The Tin Woodman set to work at once, and so sharp was his ax that the tree was soon chopped down.

They had just started to cross this odd bridge, when a sharp growl made them all look up and to their horror they saw running

toward them two great beasts with bodies like bears and heads like tigers.

"They are the Kalidahs!" said the Cowardly Lion, beginning to tremble.

"Quick!" cried the Scarecrow. "Let us cross over."

The Lion, although he was afraid, turned to face the Kalidahs, and then gave a loud and terrible

roar. The fierce beasts stopped short and looked at him in surprise. But seeing they were bigger than the Lion, the beasts also began to cross the tree.

Once they were all across, the Tin Woodman chopped off their side of the tree, and it fell, along with the Kalidahs, to the rocks below. As they walked on, they found the trees thinning, and soon enough, they came across a broad river. On the other side of the river they could see the yellow brick road.

"The Tin Woodman must build us a raft so we can float to the other side" said Dorothy. As the raft could not be completed in a day, they spent the night there.

Chapter 8

The Deadly Poppy Field

They woke up the next morning feeling refreshed and full of hope. Behind them was the dark forest they had passed safely through, and before them was a lovely, sunny country.

The raft was finally ready. Dorothy sat down in the middle of the raft and held Toto in her arms. When the Cowardly Lion stepped upon the raft, it tipped dangerously, for he was big and heavy, but the Scarecrow and the Tin Woodman stood upon the other end to steady it, and they had long poles in their hands to push the raft through the water.

When they reached the middle of the river, the swift current swept the raft downstream, farther and farther away from the road of yellow bricks. The water grew so deep that the long poles would not touch the bottom.

"This is bad," said the Tin Woodman, "for if we cannot get to land, we shall be carried into the country of the Wicked Witch of the West, and she will enchant us and make us her slaves."

"We must certainly get to the Emerald City if we can," the Scarecrow continued, and he pushed so hard on his long pole that it stuck fast in the mud at the bottom of the river. Then, before he could pull it out again—or let go—

the raft was swept away, and the poor Scarecrow was left clinging to the pole in the middle of the river.

Down the stream the raft floated, and the poor Scarecrow was left far behind. Then the Lion said, "Something must be done to save us. I think I can swim to the shore and pull the raft after me, if you will only fast to the tip of my tail."

So he sprang into the water and began to swim with all his might toward the shore. They were all tired out when they reached the shore and they also knew that the stream had carried them a long way past the road of yellow bricks that led to the Emerald City.

"We must get back to the road in some way," said Dorothy.

"The best plan will be to walk along the riverbank until we come to the road again," remarked the Lion. They walked along as fast as they could, and after a time the Tin Woodman cried out, "Look!"

Then they all looked at the river and saw the Scarecrow perched

upon his pole in the middle of the water, looking very lonely and sad. "What can we do to save him?" asked Dorothy. No one had an answer to this question.

A stork flew by and upon seeing her, Dorothy asked the stork to help save the Scarecrow. So the big bird flew into the air and over the water till she came to where the Scarecrow was perched upon his pole. Then the stork, with her great claws, grabbed the Scarecrow by the arm and carried him up into the air and back to the bank, where Dorothy, the Lion, the Tin Woodman, and Toto were sitting. When the Scarecrow found himself among his friends again, he was so happy that he hugged them all.

Soon they found themselves in the midst of a great meadow of scarlet poppies. Now it is well known that when there are many of these flowers together, their smell is so powerful that anyone who breathes it falls asleep, and if the sleeper is not carried away from the scent of the flowers, he sleeps on and on forever.

But Dorothy did not know this, and soon, her eyes grew heavy and she felt she must sit down to rest and to sleep. But the Tin Woodman would not let her do this. So they kept walking until Dorothy could stand no longer. Her eyes closed in spite of herself and she forgot where she was and fell among the poppies, fast asleep. Toto, too, had fallen down beside his little mistress. But the Scarecrow and the Tin Woodman, not being made of flesh, were not troubled by the scent of the flowers.

"Run fast," said the Scarecrow to the Lion, "and get out of this deadly flower bed as soon as you can. We will bring Dorothy with us,

but if you should fall asleep, you are too big to be carried." So the Lion ran forward as fast as he could go. In a moment he was out of sight.

The Scarecrow and the Tin Woodman picked up Toto and put him in Dorothy's lap, and then they made a chair with their hands for the seat and their arms for the sides and carried the sleeping girl and dog between them through the flowers.

They followed the bend of the river, and at last came upon their friend the Lion, lying fast asleep among the poppies, a short distance from the end of the poppy bed, where the sweet grass spread in beautiful green fields before them.

"We can do nothing for him," said the Tin Woodman sadly, "for he is much too heavy to lift. We must leave him here to sleep on forever, and perhaps he will dream that he has found courage at last."

They carried Dorothy to a pretty spot beside the river, far enough from the poppy field to prevent her breathing any more of the poison of the flowers, and waited for the fresh breeze to awaken her.

The Queen of the Field Mice

"We cannot be far from the road of yellow bricks, now," remarked the Scarecrow as he stood besides Dorothy, "for we have come nearly as far as the river carried us away."

The Tin Woodman was about to reply when he heard a low growl, and turning his head he saw a strange beast bounding over the grass toward them. It was a great yellow wildcat, and it was chasing a little gray field mouse. The Woodman raised his ax, and as the wildcat ran by, he gave it

a quick blow that cut the beast's head clean off from its body. It rolled over at his feet in two pieces.

The field mouse, now that it was freed from its enemy, came slowly up to the Tin Woodman and said in a squeaky little voice, "Oh, thank you! Thank you ever so much for saving my life. I am a Queen, the Queen of all the Field Mice!"

At that moment, several mice were seen running up as fast as their little legs could carry them, and when they saw their Queen, they exclaimed, "Oh, Your Majesty, we thought you would be killed! How did you manage to escape the Great Wildcat?"

"This friendly Tin Woodman," she answered, "killed the wildcat and saved my life. So hereafter you must all serve him, and obey his slightest wish."

"We will!" cried all the mice in a shrill chorus. And then they scampered in all directions.

Toto had awakened from his sleep and, seeing all these mice around him, he gave a bark of delight and jumped right into the middle of the group. Toto had always loved to chase mice when he lived in Kansas, and he saw no harm in it. But the mice were scared of Toto.

The Queen of the Field Mice stuck her head out from underneath a clump of grass and asked, in a timid voice, "Are you sure he will not bite us?" The Tin

Woodman assured her, and all the mice came out again.

One of the biggest mice spoke: "Is there anything we can do," it asked, "to repay you for saving the life of our Queen?"

"Oh yes, you can save our friend, the Cowardly Lion, who is asleep in the poppy bed," said the Tin Woodman.

"A Lion!" cried the little Queen. "Why, he would eat us all up."

"Oh no," declared the Scarecrow, "this Lion is a coward."

The Scarecrow told the Tin Woodman to make a truck that would carry the Lion. So the Woodman went at once to the trees and began to work. He soon made a truck out of the limbs of trees, from which he chopped away all the leaves and branches. The Scarecrow and the Tin Woodman now began to fasten

the mice to the truck, using some string they had found. One end of a string was tied around the neck of each mouse and the other end to the truck.

After a great deal of hard work, for the Lion was heavy, they managed to get him up on the truck. At first the little creatures could hardly move the heavily loaded truck, but the Woodman and the Scarecrow helped them.

Then the mice were un-harnessed from the truck and they scampered away to their homes. The Queen of the Mice was the last to leave.

Chapter 10

The Emerald City!

It was not long before they reached the road of yellow bricks, and turned again toward the Emerald City. The road was smooth, and the countryside was beautiful. Dorothy and her friends were happy to leave the dark and dangerous forest behind. But no

one came near them, nor spoke to them, because of the great Lion. The people were all dressed in clothing of a lovely emerald green color and wore peaked hats like those of the Munchkins. Dorothy remarked that this must be the Land of Oz.

"That must be the Emerald City," said Dorothy.

In front of them, and at the end of the road of yellow bricks, was a big gate, all studded with emeralds, that glittered brilliantly in the sun. There was a bell beside the door. When Dorothy rang the bell, the gate swung open and they found themselves in a high-arched room, the walls of which glistened with countless emeralds. They

were greeted by a man as short as the Munchkins, dressed from head to toe in green. Even his skin had a greenish tint to it. There was a large box beside him.

"We're here to see Oz," said Dorothy.

"It has been many years since anyone asked me to see Oz," he said with great surprise. "Oz is powerful and terrible. If your errand with him is without purpose, he could dispose of you."

"But we have come with a purpose," argued the Scarecrow. "Plus, we've been told that Oz is a good wizard."

"He is," said the green man. "He rules the Emerald City wisely. I am the Guardian of the Gates, and since you demand to see the Great Oz, I must take you to his palace. But first, you must put on the spectacles."

"Why?" asked Dorothy.

"If you do not wear spectacles, the brightness and glory of the Emerald City will blind you."

He opened the big box, and Dorothy saw that it was filled with spectacles of every size and shape. All of them had green glasses in them. The Guardian of the Gates found a pair that would fit each just right and fixed it on them.

Then the Guardian of the Gates put on his own glasses and, taking a big golden key from a peg on the wall, he opened another gate and they all followed him into the streets of the Emerald City.

In spite of the spectacles, Dorothy and her friends were dazzled by the brilliance of the city. The streets were lined with beautiful houses made of green marble and studded with sparkling emeralds. Pavements were made of green marble, too. The blocks were joined together by rows of emeralds, set closely and glittering in the brightness of the sun. The window panes were of green glass; even the sky above the city had a green tint, and the rays of

the sun were green.

All the people were dressed in green clothes, and had greenish skins. Many shops stood in the street, and Dorothy saw that all the items in the shops were green, too. Everyone seemed happy, contented, and prosperous.

The Guardian of the Gates led them through the streets until they came to a big building exactly in the middle of the city, which was the Palace of Oz, the Great Wizard. There was a soldier before the door, dressed in a green uniform and wearing a long green beard. When told about their reason for coming to the Emerald City, he said, "Step inside and I will carry your message to him."

They passed through the palace gates and were led into a big room with a green carpet and lovely green furniture set with emeralds. When they were seated, he said politely, "Please make yourselves comfortable while I tell Oz that you are here."

They had to wait a long time

before the soldier returned. When he did, he said that Oz would see them, but one on each day.

"You must remain in the palace for a few days. I will show you to rooms where you may rest in comfort after your journey."

"Thank you," replied Dorothy. "That is very kind of Oz."

Chapter 11

The Great OZ!

The next morning, they started for the Throne Room of the Great Oz.

"Are you really going to look upon the face of Oz the Terrible?" asked a green maiden who had been waiting on Dorothy.

"Of course," answered Dorothy,

"if he will see me."

"Oh, he will see you," said the soldier who had taken her message to the Wizard. "He asked me what you looked like, and when I mentioned your silver shoes, he was very interested. I also told him about the mark upon your forehead, and he decided he would admit you to his presence."

Just then a bell rang, and the green maiden said to Dorothy, "That is the signal. You must go into the Throne Room alone."

Dorothy saw a big throne of green marble that stood in the middle of the room. It was shaped like a chair, and sparkled with gems, as did everything else. In the center of the chair was an enormous head

without a body to support it or any arms or legs whatsoever. The head turned toward her and said, "I am Oz, the Great and Terrible. Who are you, and why do you seek me?"

"I am Dorothy, the Small and

Meek. I have come to you for help."

The eyes looked at her thoughtfully for a full minute. Then said the voice, "Where did you get the silver shoes?"

"I got them from the Wicked Witch of the East, when my house fell on her and killed her," she replied.

"Where did you get the mark upon your forehead?" continued the voice.

"That is where the Good Witch of the North kissed me when she bade me good-bye and sent me to you," said Dorothy.

Again the eyes looked at her sharply, and they saw she was telling the truth. Then Oz asked, "What do you wish me to do?"

"Send me back to Kansas, where my Aunt Em and Uncle Henry are," she answered earnestly.

"Well," said the head, "in this country everyone must pay for everything he gets. If you wish me to use my magic powers to send you home again, you must do something for me first."

"What must I do?" asked the girl.

"Kill the Wicked Witch of the West," answered Oz.

"But I cannot!" exclaimed Dorothy, greatly surprised.

"You killed the Witch of the East and you wear the silver shoes, which bear a powerful charm. There is now but one Wicked Witch left in all this land, and when you can tell me she is dead, I will send you back to Kansas—but not before."

Sorrowfully, Dorothy left the Throne Room.

"There is no hope for me," she told her friends sadly, "for Oz will not send me home until I have killed the Wicked Witch of the

West, and that I can never do."

The next morning the soldier with the green whiskers came to the Scarecrow and said, "Come with me, for Oz has sent for you."

So the Scarecrow followed him and was admitted into the great Throne Room, where he saw sitting on the emerald throne a most lovely lady with a pair of gorgeous wings. After he bowed down to her, she gave him a sweet smile and said, "I am Oz, the Great and Terrible. Who are you, and why do you seek me?"

The Scarecrow was expecting a large head and was surprised to see a lady. However, he answered bravely, "I come in the hope that you will give me some brains so that I will become as good as any

other man."

"I never grant favors without some return," said Oz. "Kill the Wicked Witch of the West for me, and I shall bestow upon you a great many brains."

"I thought you asked Dorothy to kill the witch," said the Scarecrow in surprise.

"So I did. I don't care who kills her. But until she is dead I will not grant your wish." The Scarecrow went sorrowfully back to his friends and told them what Oz had said.

The next morning the soldier with the green whiskers came to the Tin Woodman and said: "Oz has sent for you. Follow me."

When the Woodman entered the great Throne Room he saw neither the head nor the lady, for Oz had taken the shape of a most terrible beast.

"I am Oz, the Great and Terrible," spoke the Beast, in a voice that was one great roar. "Who are you, and why do you seek me?"

"I am a Woodman, and made of tin. Therefore I have no heart, and cannot love. I pray you to give me a heart that I may be as other men are."

Oz gave a low growl at this, but said gruffly, "If you indeed desire a heart, you must earn it."

"How?" asked the Woodman.

"Help Dorothy to kill the Wicked Witch of the West," replied the Beast. "When the witch is dead, come to me, and I will then give you the biggest, kindest, and most loving heart in all the Land of Oz."

So the Tin Woodman was forced to return sorrowfully to his friends and tell them of the terrible

Beast he had seen.

The next morning the soldier with the green whiskers led the Lion to the great Throne Room and bade him enter the presence of Oz.

The Lion saw that before the throne was a Ball of Fire so fierce and glowing, he could scarcely bear to gaze upon it. Then, a low, quiet voice came from the Ball of Fire, and these were the words it spoke:

"I am Oz, the Great and Terrible. Who are you, and why do you seek me?"

"I am a Cowardly Lion, afraid of everything. I came to you to beg that you give me courage, so that I may really become the King of Beasts, as men call me."

The Ball of Fire burned fiercely

for a time, and the voice said, “Bring me proof that the Wicked Witch is dead, and I will give you courage. But as long as the witch lives, you will remain a coward.”

He was glad to find his friends waiting for him, and told them of his terrible interview with the Wizard.

“What shall we do now?” asked Dorothy sadly.

“There is only one thing we can do,” returned the Lion, “and that is to go to the Land of the Winkies, seek out the Wicked Witch, and destroy her.”

Chapter 12

In Search of the Wicked Witch

The next morning, Dorothy asked the Guardian of the Gates, "Which road leads to the Wicked Witch of the West?"

"There is no road," answered the Guardian of the Gates. "No one ever wishes to go that way."

"How, then, are we to find her?" inquired Dorothy.

"That will be easy," replied the man, "for when she knows you are in the Land of the Winkies, she will find you, and make you all her slaves."

"Perhaps not," said the Scarecrow, "for we mean to destroy her."

"Oh, that is different," said the Guardian of the Gates. "But take care, for she is wicked and fierce, and may not allow you to destroy her. Keep to the west, where the sun sets and you cannot fail to find her."

They thanked him and turned toward the west. The Emerald City was soon left far behind. As they advanced, the ground became rougher and hillier.

The Wicked Witch of the West had but one eye, yet it was as powerful as a telescope and could see everywhere. The Wicked Witch was angry to find Dorothy and her friends in her country, so she blew upon a silver whistle that hung around her neck.

At once a pack of great wolves came running to her.

"Go to those people," said the witch, "and tear them to pieces."

"Very well," said one of the wolves, and he dashed away at full speed, followed by the others.

"This is my fight," said the Tin Woodman, "so get behind me and I will meet them as they come."

He seized his ax, which he

had made very sharp, and as the leader of the wolves came on, the Tin Woodman swung his arm and chopped the wolf's head from its body, so that it died immediately. Soon, all the wolves lay dead in a heap before the Woodman.

Then he put down his ax and sat beside the Scarecrow, who said, "It was a good fight, friend."

Dorothy thanked the Tin Woodman for saving them.

The Wicked Witch came to her balcony and saw all her wolves lying dead and the strangers still traveling through her country. This made her angrier than before, and she blew her silver whistle twice.

A great flock of wild crows flew toward her, enough to darken the sky. The Wicked Witch said to the King Crow, "Fly at once to the strangers, peck out their eyes, and tear them to pieces."

The wild crows flew in one great flock toward Dorothy and her friends. When Dorothy saw them coming, she was afraid.

But the Scarecrow said, "This is my battle, so lie down beside me and you will not be harmed."

So they all lay upon the ground, except the Scarecrow, and he stood up and stretched out his arms. When the crows saw him they were frightened, as these birds were scared of Scarecrows. But the King Crow said, "It is only a stuffed man. I will peck his eyes out."

The King Crow flew at the Scarecrow, who caught it by the head and twisted its neck until it died. And then another crow flew at him, and the Scarecrow twisted its neck also. At last, all the crows were lying dead beside him. Then he called to his friends to rise, and again they went upon their journey.

When the Wicked Witch looked

out again and saw all her crows lying in a heap, she got into a terrible rage and blew three times upon her silver whistle and a swarm of black bees flew toward her.

"Go to the strangers and sting them to death!" commanded the witch, and the bees turned and flew rapidly until they came to where Dorothy and her friends were walking. But the Woodman had seen them coming, and the Scarecrow had decided what to do.

"Take out my straw and scatter it over the little girl and the dog and the Lion," he said to the Woodman, "and the bees cannot sting them." The Tin Woodman did this, and as Dorothy lay close beside the Lion and held Toto in her arms, the straw covered them entirely.

The bees came and found no one but the Tin Woodman to sting, so they flew at him and broke off all their stings against the tin, without hurting the Tin Woodman at all. As bees cannot live when their stingers are broken, that was the end of the black bees, and they lay scattered around the Tin Woodman, like little heaps of fine coal.

Then Dorothy and the Lion got up, and Dorothy helped the Tin Woodman put the straw back into the Scarecrow again, until he was as good as ever. So they started upon their journey once more.

The Wicked Witch was so angry that she sent her slaves, the Winkies, after them. But when they neared the travelers, the Lion gave them such a ferocious and loud roar that they turned and ran back as fast as they could.

The witch decided to try one last time. She went to her cupboard and took out a Golden Cap that was studded with rubies and diamonds. This Golden Cap had a charm. Whoever owned it could call three times upon the Winged Monkeys, who would obey any order they were given. The Wicked Witch had used the charm of the cap twice already. So the Wicked Witch took the Golden Cap from her cupboard and placed it upon her head for the third time. Then she stood upon her left foot and said slowly:

"Ep-pe, pep-pe, kak-ke!"

Next she stood upon her right foot and said:

"Hil-lo, hol-lo, hel-lo!"

After this she stood upon both feet and cried in a loud voice:

"Ziz-zy, zuz-zy, zik!"

Now the charm began to work. The sun came out of the dark

sky, and the Wicked Witch was surrounded by a crowd of monkeys, each with a pair of immense and powerful wings on his shoulders. One, much bigger than the others, seemed to be their leader. He flew close to the witch and said, “You have called us for the third and last time. What do you command?”

“Go to the strangers who are within my land and destroy them all, except the Lion,” said the Wicked Witch. “Bring that beast to me, for I have a mind to harness him like a horse, and make him work.”

Some of the monkeys seized the Tin Woodman and dropped him over the rocks, where he lay so battered and dented that he could neither move nor groan.

Others caught the Scarecrow, and with their long fingers pulled the straw out of his clothes and head. They made his hat, boots, and clothes into a small bundle and threw it into the top branches of a tall tree.

The remaining monkeys threw pieces of stout rope around the Lion and wound many coils about his body and head and legs, until he was unable to bite or scratch or struggle in any way. Then they lifted him up and flew away with him to the Witch's castle, where he was placed in a small yard with a high iron fence around it, so that he could not escape.

When they turned toward Dorothy, who stood there with Toto, they dared not harm her, for she was protected by the mark of the Witch of the North. So, carefully and gently, they lifted Dorothy in their arms and carried her swiftly through the air until they came to the castle, where they set her down upon the front doorstep.

The witch was both surprised and afraid when she saw the mark on Dorothy's forehead, even more so when she saw the silver slippers. But when she saw the innocence behind the girl's eyes, she laughed to herself. "She does not know about the silver slippers and their power. I will make her my slave."

She took Dorothy to the kitchen, where she made her scrub the floor, wash the dishes, and keep the fire fed. Dorothy quietly did all that she was told to do, glad that the witch decided not to kill her. While Dorothy worked, the witch would go to where the Lion was kept and would try to harness him. But he gave such a frightening roar that she ran back and slammed the door shut. She told him that he wouldn't get anything to eat. Without her knowing, Dorothy brought food from the kitchen every night for the Lion.

Now the Wicked Witch wanted to have the silver slippers to become more powerful. She watched Dorothy closely and found out that the only time the slippers were taken off was in the night, when Dorothy would bathe. The witch dared not go in at that time, for she feared water more than anything else.

One day, when Dorothy was scrubbing the floor, the witch used her magic to put an invisible rod on the floor. Not being able to see it, Dorothy tripped and fell, and on doing so, a slipper came off. The

witch rushed forward and took the slipper, putting her own skinny foot in it.

"Give me back my slipper!" cried Dorothy, outraged.

"I will not," retorted the witch, "for it is now my slipper, not yours."

"You wicked creature! You have no right to take it from me!"

"I shall keep it just the same," said the witch, laughing at her,

"and someday, I shall get the other one from you, too."

This made Dorothy so very angry that she picked up the bucket of water that stood nearby and dashed it over the witch, wetting her from head to foot.

Instantly, the wicked woman gave a loud cry of fear, and then, as Dorothy looked at her in wonder, the witch began to shrink.

"See what you have done!" she screamed. "In a minute I shall melt away. Didn't you know water would be the end of me?" asked the witch, in a wailing, despairing voice.

"Of course not," answered Dorothy. "How could I?"

The witch gave out one final cry before melting completely. After

picking out the silver shoe, which was all that was left of the old woman, she cleaned and dried it with a cloth, and put it on her foot again. Then, she ran out to the courtyard to tell the Lion that the Wicked Witch of the West had come to an end, and that they were no longer prisoners in a strange land.

Chapter 13

The Winkies and the Winged Monkeys to the Rescue

Dorothy and the Lion went to the castle together, where she told the Winkies that they were no longer slaves.

"If our friends, the Scarecrow and the Tin Woodman, were with us," said the Lion, "I should be quite happy."

So they called the yellow Winkies and asked them if they would help rescue their friends. The Winkies said that they would be delighted. It took them two days to reach the rocky plain where the Tin Woodman lay, bent and battered. His ax was beside him, rusted, the handle gone.

The Winkies lifted him tenderly in their arms and carried him back to the Yellow Castle again.

When they reached the castle, Dorothy said to the Winkies, "Are any of your people tinsmiths?"

"Oh, yes. Some of us are very good tinsmiths," they told her.

The tinsmiths looked the Woodman over carefully and replied that they would mend him so he would be as good as ever. They worked on him for three full days and nights, at the end of which he was as good as new. The Tin Woodman, Dorothy, and the Lion had a tearful reunion. They decided to go and find the Scarecrow

next. Soon, they came to the tall tree in the branches of which the Winged Monkeys had tossed the Scarecrow's clothes.

It was a very tall tree, and the trunk was so smooth that no one could climb it, but the Woodman said at once, "I'll chop it down, and then we can get the Scarecrow's clothes."

He chopped through the tree with his new ax, until

it fell. Dorothy picked up the Scarecrow's clothes.

Back at the castle, the Winkies stuffed the Scarecrow with fresh straw until he was as good as ever! They were all happy to be with each other again, even more so that they would be able to go to Oz and get what they wanted.

Dorothy went to the Witch's cupboard to fill her basket with food for the journey, and there she saw the Golden Cap. She tried it on her own head and found that it fit her exactly. She did not know anything about the charm of the Golden Cap, but she saw that it was pretty, so she made up her mind to take it. Then, they all started for the Emerald City.

They walked on for two days, at the end of which they felt that they'd lost their way. Dorothy lost all heart then. Suddenly, she had a thought: "What if we call the field mice? Do you think they could tell us how to get to Oz?"

"I'm sure they could! Why didn't we think of this before?" said the Scarecrow.

Dorothy took a whistle from her neck that the Queen Mouse had given her and blew into it. Minutes later, the Queen stood before her and asked in a squeaky voice, "What can we do for you?"

"We have lost our way," said Dorothy. "Can you tell us where the Emerald City is?"

"Certainly," answered the Queen, "but it is a great way off, for you have had it at your backs all this time." Then she noticed Dorothy's Golden Cap and said, "Why don't you use the charm of the cap and call the Winged Monkeys to you? They will carry you to the City of Oz in less than an hour."

"I didn't know there was a charm," answered Dorothy in surprise. "What is it?"

"It is written inside the Golden Cap," replied the Queen of the Field Mice.

"Won't they hurt me?" asked Dorothy anxiously.

"Oh, no! They must obey the wearer of the Cap. Good-bye!" And she scampered out of sight with all the mice hurrying after her.

Dorothy looked inside the Golden Cap and saw some words written upon the lining. These, she thought, must be the charm, so she read the directions carefully and put the cap upon her head. After she said the charm out loud, a great chattering and flapping of wings was heard. Suddenly they were surrounded by the Winged Monkeys, their

King bowing low before Dorothy. "What is your command?" he asked.

"We wish to go to the Emerald City. Can you take us?"

"We will carry you there."

Saying this, the King and another monkey lifted Dorothy in their arms and carefully flew away. Her friends were also carried by the

Winged Monkeys, Toto being carried by one of the smaller monkeys.

As they reached the Emerald City gates, the monkeys put down their passengers gently, bowed to them, and flew away.

Chapter 14

The Discovery of Real Oz

After ringing the bell several times, it was opened by the same Guardian of the Gates they had met before. "You're back again! But I thought you went to see the Wicked Witch of the West!" he cried.

"We did," said the Scarecrow.

"And she let you go?" asked the man, in wonder.

"She could not help it, for she has melted," explained the Scarecrow.

"Melted! Well, that is good news indeed," said the man. "Who melted her?"

"It was Dorothy," said the Lion gravely.

"Good gracious!" exclaimed the man, and he bowed very low before her.

The soldier went straight to Oz and told him that Dorothy and her friends had returned. But they heard no word from him. After a few days, they sent a message with the green lady that they'd send a Winged Monkey after Oz if he didn't grant them an audience. He agreed at once, for he disliked the Winged Monkeys. He sent for them the next morning. When they entered the Throne Room, they were surprised to find it empty. Suddenly they heard a booming voice: "I am Oz, the Great and Terrible. Why do you seek me?"

"Where are you?" asked Dorothy.

"I am everywhere, but I am invisible to mortals. I will now make myself visible to you." The voice came from the throne so they all stood before it in a row.

Dorothy started by saying they had come to claim their promise.

"What promise?" asked Oz.

They each gave him their own promises. "Is the Wicked Witch truly destroyed?"

"Yes, I melted her with water," replied Dorothy.

"Oh, dear! This is quite sudden. Come back tomorrow and give me time to think."

"You've had plenty of time to think!" they cried, outraged. The Lion roared so loudly that Toto, frightened, jumped and knocked a screen over. What they all saw behind the screen shocked them. There was an old man, bald and little, who seemed pretty scared. He told them meekly that he was Oz the Terrible. "But don't strike me,

please don't, and I'll do anything you want me to."

"Then you are not a great wizard!" said Dorothy.

"Don't say it aloud! I am 'supposed' to be one. I am truly a common man," said the man.

"That's terrible! How will you give us what we asked of you?" cried the Tin Woodman.

After motioning for them to be quiet, he told them that no one knew his true identity. He showed them how he appeared to each one of them in different forms. He then told them his story.

"One day I went up in a balloon and the ropes got loose. I couldn't get down! I just sat there and floated for a long time until I came across

this beautiful country. Gradually the balloon came down. I was amidst strange people, but they seemed afraid of me, they thought I was a wizard from the clouds! So, to amuse myself, and to keep everyone busy, I told them to build a city, which they willingly did. They made a beautiful city, and I called it the

Emerald City because of all the green. One thing I feared the most was witches, for I didn't have magic in me. Fortunately, the ones in the north and south are good. But the other two were wicked. I was so happy when I heard about your house killing the Witch of the East. I was willing to promise anything so that you would kill the other witch as well. Now, shamefully, I cannot keep my word."

"I think you are a very bad man," said Dorothy.

"Oh no, my dear, I'm really a very good man, but I'm a very bad wizard, I must admit."

After hearing them plead, he finally decided to help them. He told them to come the next day, and that he would give them what they wanted. "In the meantime you shall all be treated as my guests, and while you live in the palace, my people will wait upon you and obey your slightest wish. There is only one thing I ask in return for my help: You must keep my secret and tell no one that I am a fake."

They agreed to say nothing of what they had learned, and went back to their rooms, extremely happy.

The next morning the Scarecrow said to his friends, "Congratulate me. I am going to Oz to get my brains at last. When I return I shall be as other men are." Then he said good-bye to them all in a cheerful voice and went to the Throne Room, where he rapped upon the door.

"Come in," said Oz.

The Scarecrow went in and found the little man sitting down by the window, engaged in deep thought.

"I have come for my brains," remarked the Scarecrow, a little uneasily.

"Oh, yes! Sit down in that chair, please," replied Oz. "You must excuse me for taking your head off, but I shall have to do it in order to put your brains in their proper place."

The Scarecrow told him that he wouldn't mind. Oz then emptied his head of straw and filled it with a measure of bran mixed with many pins and needles. He stuffed it into the Scarecrow's head and put straw over it to hold it in place. After replacing the head, he asked

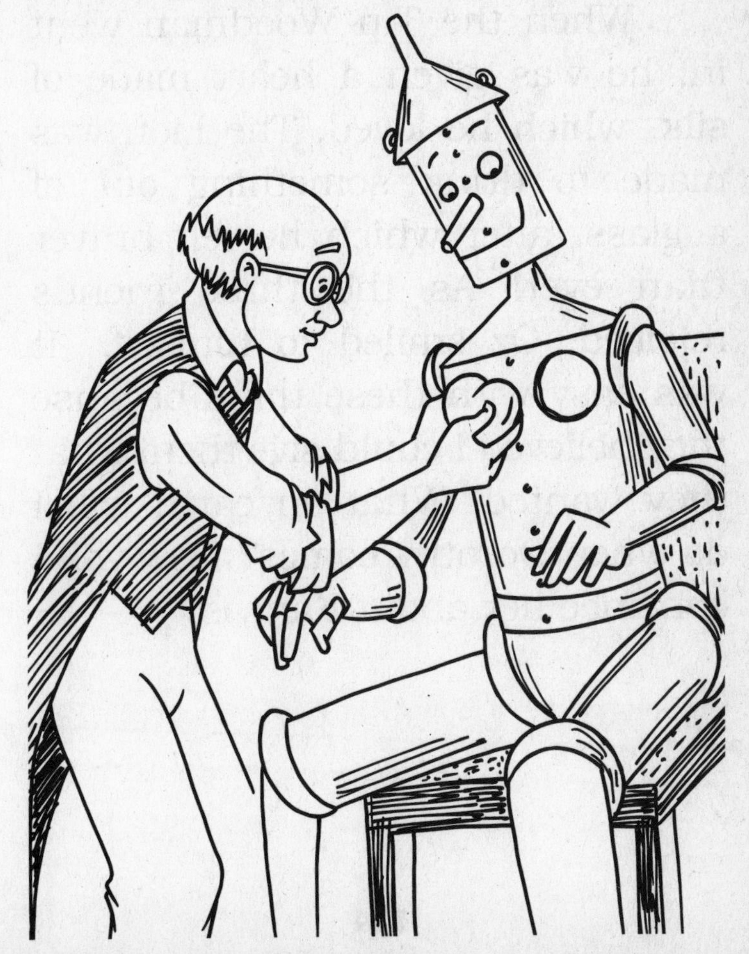

the Scarecrow how he felt. He replied that he felt very wise and sharp. The Scarecrow thanked him and went to his friends.

When the Tin Woodman went in, he was given a heart made of silk, which he loved. The Lion was made to drink something out of a glass, after which he felt braver than ever! As the three friends rejoiced, Oz smiled to himself. "It was easy with these three because they believed I could give them what they wanted. What on earth will I do when Dorothy comes? How will I convince her about Kansas?"

Chapter 15

How the Balloon was Launched

Dorothy was sent for by Oz after four agonizing days. "Sit down, my dear. I think I have found the way to get you out of this country," he said pleasantly.

"And back to Kansas?" she asked eagerly.

"Well, not exactly Kansas, but at least across the desert."

"And how do I do that?" asked Dorothy.

"When I came here, I was in a balloon. So I'm hoping that the balloon is the best way for you to get across the desert. We'll have to make a balloon of silk, coated with glue and filled with hot air. There is a lot of silk in the palace, but I'm afraid we don't have gas."

"If it won't float," remarked Dorothy, "it will be of no use to us."

"True," answered Oz. "But there is another way to make it float, which is to fill it with hot air. Though hot air isn't as good as gas, for if the air should get cold, the balloon would come down in the desert and we should be lost."

"We!" exclaimed Dorothy. "Are you going with me?"

"Yes, of course," replied Oz. "I'd much rather go back to Kansas with you and be in a circus again. Now, if you will help me sew the silk together, we will begin to work on our balloon."

So Dorothy took a needle and thread, and as fast as Oz cut the strips of silk into proper shape, the girl sewed them neatly together. It took three days to sew all the strips together, but when it was finished, they had a big bag of green silk more than twenty feet long. Then Oz painted it on the inside with a coat of thin glue to make it airtight,

after which he announced that the balloon was ready. He had a huge basket tied to it.

Once the balloon was ready, Oz sent word across the city that he was going away. He ordered the balloon to be carried out in front of the palace, and the people gazed upon it with much curiosity. The

Tin Woodman had made a fire and held the balloon over it until the hot air filled it up.

When Oz got into the basket, he told everyone that while he was away, the Scarecrow would rule over them. Just then, the ropes tying the balloon to the ground became loose. “Come, Dorothy!” cried the Wizard. “Hurry up, or the balloon will fly away.”

But Dorothy ran into the crowd, for Toto had jumped out of her arms to chase a cat. By the time she got back with Toto, the Wizard was too high in the air to get back down.

“Come back!” she screamed. “I want to go, too!”

“I can’t come back, my

dear," called Oz from the basket. "Good-bye!"

The balloon rose up into the air as everyone said good-bye, until it soon disappeared behind the clouds.

Chapter 16

Away to the South

Dorothy wept bitterly at losing her only chance to go home, but her friends consoled her.

The Scarecrow sat on the big throne, and the others stood respectfully before him.

Just then, the Scarecrow had an idea! "Call the Winged Monkeys! Maybe they can get you across

the desert."

"Why didn't I think of it earlier?" Dorothy cried, and she used the Golden Cap to call the Winged Monkeys.

"This is the second time you

have called us," said the Monkey King, bowing before the little girl. "What do you wish?"

"I want you to fly with me to Kansas," said Dorothy.

The King refused, saying that they belonged to this country and that they could not go anywhere beyond it. Saying this, they flew

away. Dorothy burst into tears.

The Scarecrow called the green-whiskered soldier into the Throne Room and asked him if he knew a way across a desert.

"I don't, but Glinda might." he said.

"Who is Glinda?" asked the Lion.

"She is the Witch of the South, the most powerful among all four witches. She rules over the Quadlings. Her castle stands at the edge of the desert, so she may be able to help you."

"How can I get to her castle?" asked Dorothy.

"It is a straight road to the south, but the road will be filled with dangerous things. This is one reason no Quadling has ever come to the Emerald City," said the soldier.

After thanking him and sending him away, they all decided to accompany Dorothy to the South.

The next morning, they traveled on until they came to a thick forest. The trees were so close to one another that it was impossible to cross the forest. Just as the Scarecrow came under the first branch, the branches twined themselves around him and the next minute, he found himself flung headlong near his friends.

Although the fall didn't hurt him, he was rather dizzy.

"The trees are trying to stop our journey!" remarked the Lion.

The Tin Woodman then walked

up to the trees and brought down his ax with such strength that he chopped the branch into two. All at once the trees began to shake as if in pain and stood straight, making way for the Tin Woodman and his friends.

They walked on until, at the edge of the forest, they came across a high wall made of white china. The surface was very smooth. The Tin Woodman decided to make a ladder so that they could climb the wall.

While the Tin Woodman made the ladder, Dorothy and the others rested. After a while, a clumsy-looking but strong ladder was made. The Scarecrow climbed up first, Dorothy supporting him so that he wouldn't fall. When they were all sitting in a row on the top of the wall, they looked down and saw a strange sight. The country that stretched before them was completely made of china. There were houses, and even

people made of china. The people were as tall as Dorothy's knee!

The Scarecrow jumped down and told the others to jump onto him, as the stuffing in him would soften the fall. They walked through the strange country and saw many strange sights.

As they walked ahead, they came across a very beautifully

dressed princess, who ran away upon seeing them. Dorothy wanted to see more of her, but she only cried, "Don't chase me! I'll fall and break myself!"

"But can you not be mended?" asked Dorothy.

"Yes, but one is not pretty again after being mended."

"But you are all so beautiful! Can I carry you back to Kansas with me and place you on Aunt Em's mantelpiece? pleaded Dorothy.

"Oh, that would make me very unhappy. Over here, we are alive and talk and move as we want. Once we are out of this country, our joints stiffen and we become still. We don't like that at all," said the princess.

"I wouldn't want to make you unhappy! I'll just say good-bye then," said Dorothy, smiling. After the princess waved good-bye, they walked across the China Country carefully until they came to another wall. It wasn't as high as the previous one. Standing on the Lion's back, they scampered over. Then, the Lion leaped over the wall himself.

Chapter 17

The Lion Becomes the King of Beasts

On the other side of the wall was a swampy, marshy-looking land. It was difficult to avoid the muddy holes and the tall grass. Somehow they made their way to solid ground. They walked for a very long time on wild and savage land, until they came across trees that were bigger and older than they had ever seen.

"This forest is perfectly delightful," declared the Lion, looking around him with joy. "Never have I seen a more beautiful place."

"It seems gloomy," said the Scarecrow.

"I would love to live here! Maybe there are wild animals in the forest," said the Lion.

They walked on until it became too dark to continue. Dorothy, Toto, and the Lion slept while the Scarecrow and the Tin Woodman stood guard. The next morning, they heard the grumble of many animals. They came to a clearing, where hundreds of wild animals had gathered. The Lion explained that a meeting was being held, and by their growls and snarls, they were all in trouble.

As he spoke, several of the beasts saw him and the crowd hushed immediately. A large tiger walked up to the Lion and bowed down to him. "Welcome, Your

Majesty! You have come at the right time. We need your help!"

"What is your trouble?" asked the Lion quietly.

"There is a fierce monster who is threatening us. It is a spider, as big as an elephant, with legs as long as tree trunks. It crawls through the forest, grabs an animal by the leg, and pulls it into its mouth. We are no longer safe."

The Lion asked if there were other lions in the forest. The tiger replied that the spider had eaten them all.

"If I kill the monster, will you accept me as your king?" asked the Lion.

"Willingly!" the animals roared.

They pointed out to the Lion where the spider was. He went there and found it sleeping. He also saw that the only delicate part of its body was the neck, very slender and long, attached to the large head. He knew it would be easier to kill it while it slept.

With one great leap he landed

on the spider's body and, with a swipe of his large paw, he cut off the spider's neck. He jumped off and watched the spider shiver to death. Once he was certain it was lifeless, he walked back to the others.

Then the beasts bowed down to the Lion as their King, and he promised to come back and rule over them as soon as Dorothy was safely on her way to Kansas.

Chapter 18

The Country of the Quadlings

Dorothy and her friends passed through the rest of the forest without any trouble. When they came out, they saw a great hill, covered from top to bottom with sharp rocks. They started to climb over the rocks carefully. Suddenly they heard a rough cry: "Keep back!"

"Who are you?" asked the Scarecrow.

A figure poked its head out from the rocks. "The hill belongs to us. No one crosses it!"

"But we have to! We need to get to the country of the Quadlings."

"You shall not!" And at that moment a very strange-looking man appeared from behind the rocks. He was short and stout, with a head like that of a hammerhead shark. He had no arms. The Scarecrow walked on, thinking the man was harmless. Just then the man's head sprang out and hit the Scarecrow, sending him sprawling backward.

"Not so easy, is it?" laughed the Hammerhead Man.

The Tin Woodman told Dorothy to call the Winged Monkeys, as she still had one chance left. She told them to take her and her friends to the country of the Quadlings.

"It shall be done," said the King. All of them were carried over

the hill, where they saw how angry the Hammerheads had become. The Winged Monkeys gently set them down in the beautiful country of the Quadlings.

"This is the last time you can summon us. Good-bye and good luck!"

They went to a farmhouse and

asked for directions to Glinda's castle. Once they got it, they made their way through the country until they came across a very beautiful castle. Before the gates were three young girls dressed in red military uniforms. As Dorothy approached, one of them asked, "Why have you come to the South Country?"

"To see the Good Witch who rules here," she answered. "Will you take me to her?"

She told the soldier girl who she was and waited when the girl went inside. She came back out to say that they could come inside.

Chapter 19

Glinda the Good Witch Grants Dorothy's Wish

When they saw Glinda, they were dazzled by her beauty. She looked far younger than her age, and she sat on a throne of rubies. She smiled kindly at Dorothy. "What can I do for you, child?"

After she heard Dorothy's story right from the cyclone till now, she laughed. "I will tell you the way back," she said. "But first you must give me the Golden Cap."

"Willingly!" said Dorothy. "I have no use for it now."

Glinda decided to use the cap three times to transport the Scarecrow, the Tin Woodman, and the Lion back to their respective kingdoms. As they thanked her, Dorothy exclaimed, "What about me? How do I get back to Kansas?"

The witch laughed and told Dorothy that she had had the power to do so all along! "Your silver slippers will carry you over the desert. If you had known about their power, you could have gone back to Kansas the very first day you arrived in Oz!"

Dorothy was speechless with shock, so the witch continued: "The silver slippers have the power to carry you to any place in the world in just three steps. All you do is knock your heels together three

times and tell the shoes where it is you want to go. You'll be there in the blink of an eye."

"If that is so," said Dorothy joyfully, "I will ask them to carry me back to Kansas at once."

She hugged and kissed all her friends good-bye and thanked them for helping her through her journey. She picked up Toto, gave them all one last teary farewell, clapped her heels together three times, and said, "Take me home to Aunty Em!"

The next thing she knew, she was sitting on the Kansas prairie, not far from where Uncle Henry was building a new home. She stood up and dusted her clothes, noticing that the silver slippers had disappeared

when she came here.

Aunty Em saw Dorothy running toward her.

"My darling child!" she cried, folding the little girl into her arms and covering her face with kisses. "Where in the world did you come from?"

"From the Land of Oz," said Dorothy gravely. "And here is Toto, too. And oh, Aunty Em! I'm so glad to be at home again!"

About the Author

Lyman Frank Baum or L. Frank Baum was born on May 15, 1856, and died on May 6, 1919. He was an American author, actor, and filmmaker.

He has often been compared to Lewis Carroll, the author of *Alice in Wonderland*, because they both had a young girl as their main character.

The Wonderful Wizard of Oz is the story of Dorothy from Kansas, who, along with her dog Toto, is transported to a magical world.

The Adventures of Tom Sawyer
The Adventures of Pinocchio
Alice in Wonderland
Anne of Green Gables
Beauty and the Beast
Black Beauty
The Call of the Wild
A Christmas Carol
Frankenstein
Great Expectations
Journey to the Center of the Earth
The Jungle Book
King Arthur and the Knights of the Round Table
Little Women
Moby Dick
The Night Before Christmas and Other Holiday Tales
Oliver Twist
Peter Pan
The Prince and the Pauper
Pygmalion
The Secret Garden
The Time Machine
Treasure Island
White Fang
The Wind in the Willows
The Wizard of Oz